THIS WALKER BOOK BELONGS TO:

_____

_____

_____

For
Richard
Woods

First published 2001 by Walker Books Ltd
87 Vauxhall Walk, London SE 11 5HJ

This edition published 2002

6 8 10 9 7 5

This book has been typeset in Garamond Book Educational

Printed in China

British Library Cataloguing in Publication Data:
a catalogue record for this book is available
from the British Library

ISBN 978-0-7445-8934-4

www.walker.co.uk

Carlo Likes Reading

Jessica Spanyol

WALKER BOOKS
AND SUBSIDIARIES
LONDON · BOSTON · SYDNEY · AUCKLAND

book

Crocodile

Snail

Elephant

Carlo reads
his bedroom.

star

books

scarf

ball

hairbrush

hair

penguin

Carlo reads the bathroom.

Carlo reads Dad.

Carlo's mum reads to Carlo.

Carlo reads to
Crackers the cat.

Carlo reads with his friend Nevil.

cloud

wall

butterfly

puddle

watering-can

flowerpot

ladybird

digger

bucket

snail

worm

baby's mum

balloon

Oper

Carlo reads
to a baby.

door

baby

pram

dummy

wheel

bakery

Price-list

pie 85p

tarts 23p

bread 47p

wedding cake

birthday cake

chocolate cake

bread

tarts

cherry pie

doughnuts

handle

sausage dogs

Pigeon

nest

bird

kitten

Carlo reads to some ducks.

hole

grass

swan

pond

duckling

crumb

duck

waterlily

Carlo reads at the market.

Carlo likes
reading
very much.

And he loves
galloping.

JESSICA SPANYOL says she wrote the first draft of **Carlo Likes Reading** with her mother when she was just six years old. "Although I loved reading I found it difficult to read when in school," she says. "Making *Carlo the Giraffe Who Could Not Read* (as it was called then) helped give me confidence."

Jessica studied Illustration at the Royal College of Art before going on to design stage sets, exhibitions and installations, working with various artists and organizations including the Royal Shakespeare Company. She has won several awards and prizes for her work.

Carlo Likes Reading, *Carlo Likes Counting* and *Carlo Likes Colours* are Jessica's first picture books for children. Carlo also appears in *Carlo and the Really Nice Librarian*. Jessica lives with her partner Richard, their son Milo and twins Lorcan and Augusta in east London.